"What time is it when twelve cats chase a mouse?"

Salem scratched his ear. He didn't know.

No matter.

He saw another line etched below the first one and assumed it was the answer. Instead, it said:

Until you answer—bad luck upon your house!

Salem felt a chill go down his spine.

What time is it when twelve cats chase a mouse?

Until you answer—bad luck upon your house!

Salem tried not to think about the Sphinx, about what happened to ancient Egyptians who couldn't answer its riddle.

"Help!" Salem mewed weakly. "I don't want to be toast!"

With that, a blinding flash of light filled the room. Salem felt someone—or some*thing*—lift his body and carry him away.

Sabrina, the Teenage Witch™
Salem's Tails™

Available from MINSTREL Books

THE KING OF CATS

Written and Illustrated by Mark Dubowski

Based on Characters Appearing in Archie Comics

And based upon the television series
Sabrina, The Teenage Witch
Created for television by Nell Scovell
Developed for television by Jonathan Schmock

A
MINSTREL®
BOOK

Published by POCKET BOOKS
New York   London   Toronto   Sydney   Tokyo   Singapore

A MINSTREL PAPERBACK *Original*

A Minstrel Book published by
POCKET BOOKS, a division of Simon & Schuster Inc.
1230 Avenue of the Americas, New York, NY 10020

Sabrina, The Teenage Witch: Salem's Tails
Based on characters appearing in Archie Comics
And the television series created by Nell Scovell
Developed for television by Jonathan Schmock

Salem quotes taken from the following episodes:
"Finger Lickin' Flu" written by Frank Coniff
"Oh, What a Tangled Spell She Weaves" written by David Weiss & Joan Binder Weiss

ISBN: 0-671-02105-2

First Minstrel Books printing January 1999

10 9 8 7 6 5 4 3 2 1

Printed in the U.S.A.

for Cathy

I learned a valuable lesson: whenever there's a crisis, I can depend on you guys—to turn on me!

—*Salem*

THE KING OF CATS

Chapter 1

Not another mouse cartoon!
Salem Saberhagen pawed the remote.

He refused to watch cartoons starring mice. They were anti-cat.

Shows like that give cats a bad name, Salem thought. *They overlook our sensitive, intelligent, neat, family-oriented, well-groomed, and extremely modest nature.*

Salem was a good example.

He bought stock only in socially re-

1

sponsible companies. Read *The New York Times*. Lived in a neat house in a good section of Westbridge, Massachusetts, with a family of three witches. Groomed his coat at least twice a day. And modest? He didn't even own a mirror.

Every now and then he *did* steal a glance at the one in the hall, which was rattling now as the front door opened and banged shut.

Sabrina Spellman was home from high school. She had mail from the box on the street in her arms as she walked into the kitchen to check the mail from the Other Realm: catalogs, a magazine, a small box, and a handful of letters. Salem padded after her into the kitchen.

No doubt the catalogs and the magazine were Sabrina's: Witchable Wearables, L.L. Scream, and *Teen Age*.

Salem could tell the box was for Aunt Zelda—a shipment from Haunted Housewares. Zelda's spells were so exotic, the ingredients were available only by mail order.

It was Aunt Hilda's turn to take care of the bills.

"The last one's for you, Salem," Sabrina said. "It's from the Metropolitan Museum of Art. I didn't know you were a member."

He had just renewed his "Friends of the Museum" membership.

"It's probably a bumper sticker," Salem said, scratching open the envelope. "Too bad I don't drive."

The envelope was addressed to "Mr. Salem Saberhagen." The museum, of course, had no idea that one of its supporters was a cat.

Not an ordinary cat, mind you. Salem

3

was a *talking* cat . . . and a *warlock* as well. Except that these days Salem's warlock powers had been taken away by the Witches' Council. They were the ones that had turned him into a cat in the first place.

It was his punishment for trying to take over the world—which was *way* against Council rules.

"Rats!" Salem said. "It's not a bumper sticker after all. Just an invitation to a sneak preview at the Westbridge Museum. Members only, black tie—and hey, the show is called *The Golden Nile.*"

"Are you going?" Sabrina asked. "I'm assuming you can still get into your tuxedo."

"I haven't put on that much weight since the last Witches' Ball," Salem said. "But no, unfortunately, I *can't* go.

4

The Sneak Preview is at the Westbridge Art Museum. Strictly N.P.A."

Which was Salemspeak for "No Pets Allowed."

Sabrina put down her magazine and looked at the museum brochure to see what he was missing.

"Wow," she said. The brochure was illustrated with photos of gold statuary, ornate jewelry, and beautifully decorated pottery.

"The Metropolitan is sending this stuff here from New York?" Sabrina asked. "That's awfully nice of them."

"It's a traveling exhibit," Salem explained. "They ship it around to other museums."

"Oh, I see," said Sabrina. "It's kind of like a 'trunk show.'" She turned her magazine around to give Salem a look at a fashion spread showing several

5

dozen dresses piled in a wooden trunk.

"New fashion designs," Sabrina told him. "Back in the old days they shipped them around in wooden trunks. They still call an out–of–New York fashion show a 'trunk show.' "

"What a clever idea," Salem said. Not the fashion designers' idea, though. Salem was talking about an idea of his own.

"I just decided I'm going to give you my ticket to *The Golden Nile,*" he announced and handed over the invitation. "Enjoy the show! You'll need something to wear, of course. Think of it as a 'golden' shopper-tunity."

"Thanks, Salem!" Sabrina said. "That's a great idea!"

Salem purred. *Poor Sabrina. She doesn't know half of what I'm really thinking!*

Chapter 2

When Sabrina told her aunts about her plan to see the *Golden Nile* exhibit, they were delighted.

"Ancient Egypt," Zelda sighed. "Those were the days." She didn't look it, but Zelda had been around for about 900 years. Plus, thanks to their ability to time travel, they even knew some of the ancient kings personally.

Salem could easily imagine Zelda hobnobbing with Egyptian royalty. Of

Sabrina's two aunts, she was the more elegant one.

But Hilda knew a few ancient rulers, too. "King Tut was cute," she said. "Did you know he became the head honcho when he was only nine years old?" Salem could imagine Hilda and Tut out on the town.

"I guess the voting age was a lot lower back then," Sabrina said.

"My, you *do* have a lot to learn about ancient Egypt, don't you?" said Zelda. "They didn't have elections back then. I'm sure you'll find the museum's exhibit very educational."

"Oh, it'll be a lot of fun, too," Hilda said with a perky grin. "Do avoid the Mummy's Curse, however. It's *extremely* bad luck to pick that up on a Friday."

"Did someone say bad luck?" Salem

said. Being a black cat made him extra sensitive to things like that.

"Nothing personal, Salem," Hilda said.

"There's a very good reason behind the Mummy's Curse," Zelda explained. "When an Egyptian king—called a pharaoh—was laid to rest, his tomb was filled with treasures that his followers thought he could use in the next life."

"But other people thought they could use the king's treasures in *this* life," Hilda added.

"Robbers, you mean," Salem said.

"Right," Zelda continued. "To scare the robbers, the servants of the king made up stories about a curse. According to them, bad luck would befall anyone who disturbed the mummy's tomb."

"Some people were still tempted, of course," Hilda said. "All that gold . . ."

"Oh, please," Salem moaned. "Can

9

we change the subject?" He really wanted to go to the sneak preview.

He was dying to see all that gold.

Salem loved money almost as much as the sound of a can opener.

Sabrina and her aunts understood how disappointed he was that he couldn't go to the show. But there was nothing they could do about it. Pets were not allowed in the museum. Salem was not allowed by the Witches' Council to speak to mortals, either. And where would he carry his invitation—in his mouth? That was bad manners.

They didn't mention it again in front of Salem until the night of the show when Sabrina was all ready to go.

"I really wish you were going, too, Salem," Sabrina said. She stood in the front hall waiting for Hilda, who was getting her keys.

"That dress looks terrific on you," Salem said, playing the good sport. "Like you just stepped out of a *trunk* show."

There was just a hint of sadness in his eyes. At least, that's the way Salem wanted it to look. Otherwise they'd get suspicious.

"Don't forget your camera, Sabrina," Hilda said as she came downstairs jangling her keys.

"Oops!" Sabrina zipped past Hilda on the stairs and went into her room.

Hilda gave Salem a kind smile.

"Sabrina will tell you all about it, sweetie," she said. "And she'll take pictures."

Oh, whoop-dee-do! Salem thought. *Thanks a lot. How exciting—not.*

11

He only said aloud, "Thanks a lot."

A minute later Sabrina was back with her camera, and they all headed for the car.

Hilda and Sabrina got in the front seat and waved good-bye to the brave little cat in the driveway.

"Thanks again, Salem," Sabrina called. He looked really pitiful standing there all alone.

Salem knew it, too. He sniffed back a tear, loudly, betting on the long shot that they would take him after all.

"Rules are rules," Hilda said with a sad smile, as Sabrina leaned out to shut the car door.

"Wait a minute, Hilda," Salem called out, *hold it right there.* "Is this the car you took grocery shopping?"

Hilda gave him a blank look. "I guess so," she said. "I mean . . . sure."

12

"The reason I ask," Salem went on, "is that I couldn't find the *tuna* in the pantry. Did you remember to get tuna?"

"Of course—two big cans, just like you wanted," she told him.

"Hmmmm!" Salem said. He knew she was going to say that. "I wonder if they *spilled out of the bag*? Maybe they're *still in the trunk!* Mind if I have a look?"

Hilda frowned. "Okay, but hurry, Salem. We don't want to be late." Hilda reached under the dashboard and pulled the lever that opened the trunk lock from inside.

Salem held back a cheer. *Yes!* His plan was working.

He went around to the back of the car and hopped onto the rear bumper. The trunk was empty except for the

spare tire, a can of car wax, and a car-washing sponge. Salem clawed the sponge and stuffed it into the trunk lock, jamming it.

"Find it?" he heard Hilda say.

"What? Oh, the tuna!" He almost forgot. "No, it's not here! I'll check in the house again!"

"Close the trunk, will you?" Hilda yelled back.

Salem reached up and pulled the trunk lid down, *from the inside*—and Hilda turned out of the driveway.

"Bye, Salem!" he heard Sabrina call out the car window.

Bye! Not!

CHAPTER 3

When the Spellmans got to the museum, people were already lined up at the door. A tall security guard with a bushy mustache was checking invitations at the entrance.

"This is *so* cool!" Sabrina said. Everyone was dressed up, and velvet ropes lined the walkway. It felt like a visit to a palace.

In a way, it was. The museum had designed the exhibit to resemble a walk through an ancient palace.

15

The objects on display were recovered from tombs. But they had originally come from palaces. They had been buried with their royal owners deep inside the pyramids.

Deep inside the trunk of Hilda's car, Salem was listening for signs that they were getting close to the museum. Eventually, with his super cat hearing, he heard Hilda say they'd arrived.

"I'll pull up in front of the museum and wait there until you get inside," he heard Hilda tell her niece. "Then we'll be back in an hour."

"Great, Aunt Hilda. Thanks again."

The second he heard her door handle click Salem pushed up the trunk lid. It hadn't closed all the way, thanks to the sponge trick. Then he shot out under the lid, sailed over the bumper, sprang off the curb, and streaked for a neatly clipped row of bushes along the front wall of the museum.

He was under the shrubs in seconds flat, checking his escape route to see if anyone had spotted him. *Everything's under control,* he thought. Sabrina was distracted by the museum crowd. Hilda had gotten out to slam the trunk shut, but she seemed unsuspecting, too. The rest would be easy.

I'll just give the guard the slip and then enjoy the show!

The important thing for Salem was to get in fast, during the reception. That was when the guests would have refreshments. *For as long as they're at the refreshment tables, I'll have the exhibit halls to myself,* Salem figured. After he'd seen the collection, he'd make an early exit and wait in front of the museum for Hilda to show up again.

I wonder how I'm going to get back in Hilda's trunk, Salem thought. He'd think of something. Cats had a way of landing on their feet, no matter what. He pounced from his hideout in the bushes and landed lightly behind a big stone flower pot at the top of the museum's front steps. The guard taking tickets was just on the other side.

Salem watched a few more guests arrive, show their invitations, and walk in.

He was waiting for just the right person to arrive.

A woman. A woman in a big, flowing dress.

Here she comes, Salem thought, and he ran to hide under her dress. *It's like being under a tablecloth in here,* Salem thought as he stepped lightly behind her heels, underneath the flowing gown. Salem stopped when the lady stopped to show her invitation.

As soon as they got inside, Salem dashed off.

CHAPTER 4

*T*oo *bad the Westbridge Art Museum doesn't allow roller-skating,* Salem thought. *The front lobby is perfect for it.*

The empty marble floor of the lobby was as smooth as glass. A grand staircase curved up from the center to the second floor.

The galleries were at the other end of two hallways off the main lobby. For the night of the preview, the hallway to the left was set up with refreshment tables, and that's where all the guests were. Salem skulked along the wall and took the other hallway.

A sign posted just inside said he was entering the Hall of Pyramids.

All along the walls were large framed photographs of the Pyramids—the final resting places of ancient Egypt's royal families.

Where the main hallway ended and the galleries began, Salem stopped to admire an enlarged photograph of the giant Sphinx. It had to be Salem's favorite statue.

To the Egyptians who carved it, it was probably the portrait of a pharaoh. The pharaoh's head had been transplanted onto the body of a lion—a giant cat—to make a point about the pharaoh's greatness.

Which made a lot of sense to Salem.

Two thousand years after that, the ancient Greeks misunderstood the whole thing—or pretended to, anyway. They decided that the monument represented the Sphinx from their own myth about a woman with a lion's body and a twisted sense of humor. She asked a riddle, *and if you didn't know the answer,* Salem remembered, *you were toast.*

Salem looked in both directions for security guards before crossing into the next hallway, which the museum had decorated with hieroglyphics—the Egyptians' picture-writing system.

This is amazing, Salem thought. In his full-powered warlock days, Salem had cooperated with a pharaoh in his plan to take over the world, and he could read hieroglyphics. *There's not a single spelling error on this entire wall.*

Then he entered the Room of Jars.

The museum's Room of Jars looked like a Los Angeles pottery shop after a small earthquake. The jars were chipped and cracked, but they were neatly shelved and the picture-writing on them was still cheery and bright after five thousand years.

Only a single jar was in perfect condition.

Hey, look at that, Salem thought when he saw how it was decorated. *It's a dozen cats!* At first he thought they were dancing. Then he decided not. They were running. They were chasing something. Salem padded around the jar and on the other side he found—

—a mouse.

And above the mouse a riddle was

23

etched in picture-writing. Salem read it aloud.

"What time is it when twelve cats chase a mouse?"

Salem scratched his ear. He didn't know.

No matter.

He saw another line etched below the first one and assumed it was the answer. Instead, it said:

Until you answer—bad luck upon your house!

Salem felt a chill go down his spine.

What time is it when twelve cats chase a mouse?

Until you answer—bad luck upon your house!

Salem was trying not to think about the Sphinx, about what happened to ancient Egyptians who couldn't answer its riddle.

"Help!" Salem mewed weakly. "I don't want to be toast!"

With that, a blinding flash of light filled the room.

Salem felt someone—or some*thing*— lift his body and carry him away.

At first he was afraid. He kept his eyes shut tight.

Then he heard a voice, gentle and kind. It was calling his name.

". . . Saaa-lem . . ." It sounded like the voice of an angel.

And Salem was not afraid anymore. *I've had a good life*, he thought, *I'm thankful for that.*

The voice spoke to him again, calling his name, ". . . Saaaaaa-lem . . ."

Salem felt she could hear his thoughts. *I just have one request—tell*

25

me the answer to the riddle. Please.
Whoever, whatever you are. What time
is it when twelve cats chase a mouse?

Salem opened his eyes so the voice
could reveal itself—and the answer to
the riddle—to him. Spots of colored
light floated in front of his eyes. Then a
face appeared.

"Sabrina?" Salem croaked.

Salem was confused. For some reason
he seemed to be all right. Sabrina was
there. He was safely curled in her arms.
He looked around. They were sur-
rounded by gold cat statues wearing
precious jewelry.

"Why am I here?" he whispered.
"And why are those *other* cats here?
And why are *you* here? And *where is*
here in the first place?"

"We're in the Westbridge Art Museum," Sabrina reminded him. "This

room is called the Lair of the Cats. I brought you here when I found you in the Room of Jars. Do you remember being there?"

"I remember the jars all right," Salem said.

"You were passed out in the middle of the room!"

"It's all coming back to me now," Salem said. Then he told Sabrina what had happened.

That he'd read a riddle on the jar with twelve cats chasing a mouse.

That he couldn't come up with the answer.

That the jar said he was under a curse until he did.

And that the jar had already tried to toast him with a lightning bolt. It flashed from behind the riddle jar.

Sabrina rolled her eyes. She knew

what happened. "That flash wasn't a lightning bolt! It was my camera! I took a photo of that jar right before I found you! Don't try to distract me with a crazy story, anyway, Salem—I'm mad at you! You sneaked in here, didn't you!"

Now Salem felt extra bad (because he'd been caught).

Caught between the riddle of the jar and wrath of Sabrina, he told himself. *Now I'm doomed for sure.*

So Salem did what he always did when he was in a really tough situation. He switched to Plan B.

Plan B meant Begging.

"Pleeeeeeease," he moaned softly. "Please help me, Sabrina."

Sabrina frowned. Salem knew she hated it when he begged.

"Help me . . ." he croaked miserably.

Hated it because it *always worked*.

"Okay, Salem," she said at last. "I'll help you."

I love groveling, Salem thought. *When it works.*

"The riddle on the jar is just for fun, anyway, Salem," Sabrina assured him. "Remember what Aunt Zelda said about the Mummy's Curse—that was all made up."

Salem didn't think they were connected. "The riddle on the jar isn't to scare robbers, Sabrina. I feel that I may actually be doomed."

"You're not doomed," Sabrina said. "Silly, yes. But not doomed."

Sabrina's confidence made Salem feel a little better.

"Come on, let's get you out of here," she said. "We'll use a back exit or something. It's almost time to meet Aunt Hilda anyway."

29

Sabrina carried Salem out of the Lair of Cats and into the Waters of the Nile, a corridor with a display of carved figures that showed how early Egyptians fished in the Nile River and grew corn in the river's valley.

A sign marked "detour" pointed the way around a plywood partition. It was like going backstage behind the exhibits. They followed a narrow unpainted hallway that came to a dead end with a door. The door opened on a stairwell that went into a basement where Salem led the way in the dark over wooden crates that were evidently in storage.

"I feel like I'm in a tomb," Sabrina whispered.

"Don't say that!" Salem shot back. The place was scary enough just being a basement.

But soon Salem found a door, and

when Sabrina managed to push it open they found themselves outside on a concrete platform.

"We're in the back of the museum," Sabrina said. They were on the loading dock.

"Okay, we'll just circle around," Salem said. A few minutes later they found the front of the museum again, but they were trapped inside a tall fence.

"Can you climb it?" Salem said.

"Not in this dress," Sabrina told him. "But that's okay." She waggled her finger and said:

"Fences tall, fences wide,
Put us on the other side!"

In the blink of an eye they were.

"I hope no one saw that," Salem worried.

31

"Oh, don't panic," Sabrina said.

"Under normal circumstances, I wouldn't," Salem told her. "But you forget, I'm *doomed*."

"I'm not going to listen to talk like that," Sabrina said. "Anyway, there's our car."

The aunts were stuck in traffic halfway up the block.

"Come on, I'll carry you," she said. Salem sprang into her arms and they stepped toward the curb.

And got stopped—by a whole gang of museum guards. A wall of blue uniforms stood in their way.

"Told you I was doomed," Salem whispered. "That fence you whammed was probably wired!"

Sabrina shook her head. The guards were stopping everyone, not just them. They were holding everyone on the sidewalk to give the traffic on the street a chance to clear.

The guard nearest to them was even smiling. It was the one from the front door. The one with the bushy mustache.

"Kitty-kitty!" he said, giving Salem a scratch between the ears. The man obviously liked cats.

I hope what I've got isn't contagious, Salem thought.

When the traffic cleared the guards let everyone go and Sabrina caught up with Hilda at the curb.

Salem was still trying to prove he was doomed. "It's bad luck getting stopped by security guards for any reason, Sabrina," he argued as they climbed into the back seat.

"Wrong," Sabrina said, buckling his seat belt. "It was *good* luck we didn't

run into security guards *earlier,* when I was casting a spell on that fence."

Hilda and Zelda, of course, were just amazed to see Salem.

"I'll explain everything," Sabrina promised them. "Salem couldn't resist the sneak preview, and then he had a little scare, but everything's fine now."

Then Hilda pulled away from the curb, and they all felt the car leaning in a strange way. "It feels like we're dragging something," Hilda said. She pulled back to the curb and flicked on the emergency flasher and got out to have a look.

They had a flat tire.

"I knew it," Salem said.

The air hissing from the hole in the tire sounded to him a lot like the hissing of twelve angry cats.

CHAPTER 5

Don't get *near me!*" Salem cried.

A whole day had gone by since Salem's visit to the museum, so Sabrina was surprised to see he still had the jitters.

Salem was more sure than ever that the riddle on the jar was controlling his life.

"I've had nothing but bad luck all day! I really am doomed!" he whined.

"I think you're overreacting just a little bit," Sabrina said, letting him know she wasn't in the mood for doom. She had six pages of math homework to do and a bad case of the hair frizzies, too.

"This is serious!" Salem insisted. "You've got to help me figure out what time it is when twelve cats chase a mouse! It's your house, too," he pleaded, reminding her, "The jar said bad luck upon your *house*."

Sabrina made a stab at answering the riddle. "Time to get a new *mouse*? No, that's dumb," she said. "By the way, where are all the glasses?" she said, getting off the subject.

None in the cabinet or the sink.

Without a word, Salem pointed a paw at a pile of broken glass on the floor at the end of the counter.

"You broke a glass?" Sabrina said.

She was surprised. Usually he was so careful. "Actually, it looks like you broke several."

"It's more than several," Salem told her. "I broke *every* glass in the house!"

Sabrina was stunned.

"It was really bad luck," Salem moaned. "I was trying to peel an orange for Hilda."

Sabrina frowned. "How can you break every glass in the house while peeling an orange?"

"Well, first of all Zelda washed them. The glasses I mean, not the oranges. I was watching her because I was bored. There's really nothing to do around here all day except housework, and naps, and claw maintenance, you know."

Sabrina encouraged him to get on with it. "And then . . ."

"And then she left the glasses out on the counter to dry." Salem's voice cracked and a tear rolled down his cheek. "I was over by the sink. I was just taking a little break. Peeling an orange for Hilda—you know how she loves them. Anyway, my paw slipped. The orange bounced off the cabinet, landed on the counter, and rolled a perfect strike, right down the middle of the glasses."

Sabrina imagined the crash. "I didn't know you could bowl," she said, pointing her finger at the pile of broken glass.

"One, two, just like new."

The glasses magically went back together and tucked themselves away in the cabinet.

"I've never rolled a perfect strike in my *life*," Salem cried. "It wasn't beginner's luck, either—it was *bad* luck. I'm telling you, it's the riddle!"

What happened to the glasses was bad enough, but it wasn't the only thing.

Lots of things had gone wrong for Salem while Sabrina and her aunts had been away during the day.

The washing machine had overflowed.

The mail truck had backed over the mailbox.

And all the smoke alarms in the house had gone off at once, for absolutely no reason.

"I'm still not convinced you're doomed," Sabrina told him. "But just in case, I'd like you to stay away from my room for a few days."

Salem pouted.

"Especially don't go near my mirror." Sabrina had barely made it through her own seven days of bad luck the last time she broke a mirror.

Salem moaned.

"Oh, cheer up," Sabrina said. "If it *is* true, and the jar *is* controlling you, Zelda and Hilda will know what to do," she said.

Salem's jaw dropped. "When you told them what happened at the museum, they said their flat tire wasn't enough evidence. They wouldn't be having second thoughts, now, would they?"

"Well, when they see the mailbox, and the washing machine, and hear about the smoke alarms, and the glasses, well, I don't know . . ." Sabrina teased. But Salem didn't think it was funny.

"Relax," she said. "I'm sure one of them has an anti-riddle spell or two up her sleeve."

"And what if they *don't*?" Salem demanded.

"Then they'll whip up something new," Sabrina said.

But Salem knew she was only guessing. "What if they *can't*?" he said.

Sabrina shrugged. "Well, I don't know," she said. "What do you think?"

Salem shuddered.

"I'll tell you what I think," he said grimly. "I think they're going to make me an outside kitty."

He was looking her square in the eye.

But Sabrina just thought that was funny. "Outside kitty!" She giggled. "What's that?"

If Sabrina wasn't right about everything, she was right about *one* thing.

There was no way to hide Salem's accidents from Hilda and Zelda.

The aunts hadn't been home for fifteen minutes before they'd noticed *everything* that had gone wrong.

First Zelda noticed the smoke detector in the hallway. Its cover was open. "What happened here?" she asked.

Then Hilda noticed the floor was damp around the washing machine. "And what's this mess?" she asked.

Of course, both of them had noticed the mailbox. "And what happened to the mailbox?" they asked.

Before Salem could explain, Zelda commented about the glasses. They had been put away in the cabinet upside down. Hilda and Zelda always put them away right side up.

Sabrina wasn't surprised. She suspected grown-ups had some kind of strange sixth sense about things like this.

What surprised Salem was that when he told them what had happened, neither of Sabrina's aunts was angry about it.

"Salem, it's *no problemo*," Hilda laughed, borrowing one of Salem's favorite lines.

"You mean you're not mad?" Salem said.

"Of course not!" Zelda said. "We have *spells*, remember?"

"Then you guys *do* have an anti-riddle spell," Sabrina crowed. "What did I tell you, Salem!"

"That's not what I mean, Sabrina," Zelda warned. "We have spells to take care of household emergencies. There is no magic cure for riddles."

"We wish there *were*," Hilda said.

"Because they're so corny?" Sabrina guessed.

"No, because they're so *strong*," Hilda explained. "Witches have been looking for the cure for riddles longer than cats have been looking for the cure for fleas!"

"That is an *incredibly* long time," Salem admitted.

"Thousands of years," Zelda smiled.

Now Sabrina was really worried. "If witches have been looking for the cure for riddles for thousands of years, then you probably won't be whipping up something anytime soon . . . ?"

"I'm afraid not, Sabrina. And stop biting your nails," Zelda said gently.

Salem put down his paw. "How can you two be so happy-go-lucky?" he wanted to know. They weren't taking this seriously enough for him.

Zelda smiled calmly. "Well, think about it! We *are* only talking about a *riddle!*"

Hilda grinned. "And every *riddle* has an *answer!*"

Salem shook his head sadly. "Not this one. Let me remind you that this little gem happens to come from a jar that's almost five thousand years old. Where in the world do you think you can find the punch line to a joke *that's five thousand years old?*"

"I know," Hilda kidded. "The comedy club downtown. I've seen some acts there that are really quite ancient . . ."

"How about that fellow on TV after the eleven o'clock news?" Zelda asked. "He's been repeating the same jokes for years and years!"

"You mean the guy on channel—" Hilda started to say.

"No, the other guy," Zelda said.

Salem hung his head. It seemed impossible to him. As a matter of fact, it *was* impossible—for him. But it was *not* impossible for Hilda or for Zelda.

"All we have to do is take a little trip to Egypt," Hilda explained.

"Ancient Egypt, of course," Zelda added. She looked at Sabrina apologetically. "That means you'll have to wait here, Sabrina. Tomorrow's a school day."

Sabrina could time-travel as well as any witch. But her aunts restricted her time travel on school days. Even though they could return to the same moment in time that they left, they could be in ancient Egypt for hours, or even days. Sabrina could come back exhausted. This time, they could handle the job without her. Sometimes being a teenage half-witch had its drawbacks.

Sabrina shrugged. "I'll hold down the fort," she said cheerfully, giving Salem a pat on the head. "Have a nice flight, Salem. Egypt five thousand years ago is a long trip—think of all the temporal transit frequent flier miles you'll rack up."

Salem smiled weakly. "Well, lucky me."

"Shiver, shiver, Nile River."

When Hilda said that, she, Zelda, and Salem vanished from the kitchen in Westbridge, Massachusetts, and shot southeast across the sky over the Atlantic Ocean, headed for the continent of Africa and the banks of Egypt's famous Nile River.

"Golden arrows, time of pharaohs!"

47

When Zelda said that they arrived, perfectly dressed for shopping, at a busy street market of Cairo, 3000 B.C.

"The caftans are remarkably cool, don't you agree?" Zelda said.

"Oh yes," said Hilda. "And doesn't Salem look cute!"

"I feel silly wearing a hankie on my head," Salem said about the wrapped-cloth headgear that had appeared on his head. "And these bloomers are itchy." He hopped into Hilda's arms to avoid being stepped on by a yak. The only places it wasn't wall-to-wall people it was wall-to-wall animals.

Salem had never smelled anything like it.

"Kind of like Westbridge Mall meets Noah's Ark," he pointed out.

Hilda paid no attention to his complaining. "You know what I love about this place? The bargains! The last time I was here you could buy things for *peanuts!*"

"That's because they haven't invented money yet," Zelda said.

Salem sensed the making of an all-day shopping trip for Hilda, and it made him impatient. "Can we please get down to business?" he panted. "According to the riddle jar in the museum, if I don't answer the question 'What time is it when twelve cats chase a mouse,' I'm doomed. Doomed! Let's stay focused, shall we?"

"Oh, stop it, Salem," Zelda said. "Calm down. There's time to be focused *and* shop!"

"You just convinced me, Zelda. The jar is right. I really *am* doomed."

"Nobody's *doomed*, Salem," Zelda said, giving him a pat on the head. "Ev-

erything is going to be all right, just as
soon as we find Cheap Cheops."

"Oh, he's fabulous," Hilda said gaily.
"You'll love him! He's got almost everything you'd ever want—including the
answers to ancient riddles! And why do
you think they call him *Cheap*?"

Salem said he couldn't imagine. "And
I really don't want to know."

"Oh, look, there's his picture!" Zelda
called. She pointed to a banner waving
over the heads of the crowd.

The banner showed a man wearing a
white bandanna and a grin that
stretched from ear to ear. "CHEAP
CHEOPS!" it read in bold lettering
above his head. "TRY IT, YOU'LL
LIKE IT!"

"His real name's Shadrack," Hilda
whispered. "Cheops comes from the
name of a famous pharaoh."

Salem rolled his eyes. "You're placing my future in the hands of a discount street peddler with a fake name whose advertising slogan is 'Try it, you'll like it?' Yes, ladies and gentlemen, I really am doomed."

"Oh, chill, will you?" Hilda said.

"I'd love to," Salem crabbed. "But let me point out that the temperature is something like one hundred and ten degrees here—and I'm wearing a real fur coat!"

Gradually they made their way through the crowd to a table where the man whose portrait was on the banner was accepting a chicken as payment for a rug.

"Yoo-hoo! Hello, Shad!" Zelda called out over the other shoppers, using his real name.

When he spotted Hilda and Zelda his

smile widened. He hailed them both in a foreign language, then he winked and spoke again, this time in perfect modern English.

"Whuzzup!"

That made Salem feel better. Shad, as Zelda called him, was not an out-of-date shopkeeper after all. The way he'd said hello had Salem convinced that Cheap Cheops had done some serious time-traveling himself. He even had that certain warlock look . . .

"Be with you in a minute," he said. Then he ducked under the table and came up with a sack made of rough paper.

"Papyrus okay?" he said, asking a lady with an oil lamp if she wanted a bag. She nodded, and Cheops cheerfully helped her pack it up. It was funny— she already had more bags than she could comfortably carry. It looked as if she'd bought something from every shop in the market.

Shadrack turned to Hilda and winked. "Tourists!" he chuckled. "Now, how can I help you today?"

"Have you met Salem?" Hilda said, showing him the cat in her arms. "He used to be a warlock, too. Then there was this little disagreement with the Witches' Council—and they had to turn him into a cat for a while."

"Tried to take over the world, didn't you?" Shadrack smiled sympathetically. "Only mortals are allowed to attempt that," he said. "A cat, huh? I think I'm allergic to cats—"

"It's only temporary," Salem told him. "I get turned back into a warlock after I serve one hundred years."

"That'll be over with before you know it," Shad agreed.

"Anyway," Zelda said, "the problem we're having has to do with a riddle. Salem accidentally read one in the museum."

Shadrack groaned. "Don't tell me. Is it the one that goes 'What's black and white and red all over?' "

"Everybody knows that one," Hilda said. "A newspaper."

"Hot fudge sundae with ketchup on it," Zelda said.

"Zebra with a suntan," Shad laughed, then sneezed.

"All right already!" Salem moaned. "I need the answer to 'What time is it when twelve cats chase a mouse?' "

"Hm." Shad stroked his chin, thinking. "Time to get a new mouse? No, that's dumb. Let me see what I've got." He ducked under the table again and came up with a wooden box.

Shad placed the box down carefully

54

on the table. Then he unhooked his ear-ring, on which hung a tiny key. He used the key to open the box and showed them what was inside: several rows of tiny pottery jars with cork stoppers.

"Answers to riddles," he explained, rubbing his eyes. "Very valuable."

He checked the contents label on three of them before he found what he was looking for.

"Here it is: What time is it when twelve cats chase a mouse?" he said. "Open the bottle and listen for the answer to come out. Don't forget it—for security purposes, these things are not written down. And that's my last one for that particular riddle. So be careful."

But just as he handed it over to Hilda, Shad sneezed again and the bottle flew from his hand. Zelda and Hilda both tried to catch it, but they missed.

The bottle fell to the street and shattered.

In the confusion, no one heard the answer slip out.

At first no one said a word. They just stared at the little crumbs of hard clay on the dusty street.

Finally Shadrack spoke.

"An unfortunate turn of events. Can I interest you in a collectible Beanie Mummy doll?"

CHAPTER 6

Back together in Westbridge again, Hilda and Zelda and Salem and Sabrina all tried to adjust to life with Salem's bad luck.

They packed away the good dishes and ate off paper plates.

They wore headlight-reflecting jogging suits at all times.

They started every day with a fire drill.

And they put up around the house

every kind of safety poster. How to save a person who was choking. How to identify poisonous snakes and spiders. How to dial 911. How to send an SOS. How to make smoke signals that say, "Help, I fell down and I can't get up!"

"You know, this safety stuff kind of grows on you after a while," Zelda said. She was checking out her new look—a pair of welder's goggles on her head—in the new stainless-steel mirror in the hall.

"Yeah, you get used to it, you know?" Sabrina agreed in a muffled voice, speaking through her gas mask.

"And the anti-fire sprinkler system we put in is supposed to add a lot to the value of the house, I understand," said Hilda. "Not to mention those lifeboats."

But no matter how careful they were,

crazy things and bad luck accidents kept happening around the Spellman house.

Sometimes the bad luck made everyone laugh. Like when Zelda's computer quit working and just played the Weather Channel all day. Other times it made everyone cry, like when the dryer shrunk all their clothes to toddlers' size 1. Eventually, it made everyone mad.

Mad at Salem.

Finally, Hilda put her foot down. (Zelda would have put her foot down too, but it was sprained from a fall.)

Maybe it was that mishap involving the blender in the kitchen, the spoon in the blender, and the chandelier in the hall. (How was Salem supposed to know the blender was already switched on when he plugged it in?)

Or maybe it was that problem with the electric garage door opener and Zelda's new car. (When the door came down at the wrong time it mainly scratched the roof of the car, where no one looked; so why was she so upset?)

Or the accident with the fingernail polish and Hilda's violin case. (Salem didn't even want to think about that one.)

One of those accidents was the last straw.

One of those accidents was the one accident that turned Salem from an inside kitty, who lived in the house, into *(gulp!)* an outside kitty, who lived in the yard.

For a cat like Salem, it was a fate worse than death.

Sabrina found out about it the afternoon she came home from school and couldn't find him in his usual spot in the kitchen.

"What are you doing out here?" she said when she finally discovered him moping on the back porch.

"Oh, you know, just getting some fresh air," Salem said.

"I can always tell when you're fibbing, Salem," Sabrina said. "Your mouth is moving."

That wasn't exactly true, but Salem let it go.

"Come on, tell me the truth," she said.

Salem hung his head. "I'm an outside kitty now," he choked. "Aunts' orders!"

Bitter tears dripped onto the deck.

"What exactly does that mean?" Sabrina wanted to know.

Salem looked at her as if she'd just asked him which way was up.

"An outside kitty," he explained firmly, "is a kitty who can't come inside . . . ever!"

"You mean the *house* is N.P.A.?" Sabrina gasped.

"That's right," Salem growled. "No pets allowed. For me that means no more TV, no more phone calls, no more between-meal snacks . . ."

"Kind of like being grounded, only sort of just the opposite," Sabrina commented.

"Exactly," Salem said. "As an outside kitty, I can now go *anywhere and everywhere I don't want to.*"

Just then they heard a rumbling noise. A fresh breeze blew across the yard and big drops of rain slapped on the porch.

Salem shook his head. "Have you

ever noticed how often it actually *rains* in Westbridge?" he said.

Sabrina went inside to get him an umbrella.

CHAPTER 7

Sabrina did her best to make Salem more comfortable outside, but nothing really worked.

"The only thing that can make me happy is finding the answer to that riddle," Salem told her. "I've got to find out what time it is when twelve cats chase a mouse!"

Sabrina was hopeful. "We're all working on it, Salem," she said. "Just yesterday Zelda came up with 'time to get rid of some of the cats.' I know it's not the right answer, but at least she was trying."

Salem pouted. "She *would* come up with an answer like that," he said. "She got rid of *me!*"

"I was up last night until after twelve trying to come up with the answer myself," Sabrina sighed.

For the next minute they both just sat there thinking.

A leaf fell from a tree.

A bird hopped off the fence and pecked in the grass.

Somewhere a car door slammed.

"What did you say?"

Sabrina looked up. "Hm?"

Salem reached up and placed his front paws on her chest, looking her square in the eye. "After I said Zelda got rid of me. What did you say?

Something about the time. Tell me, *exactly*."

Sabrina tried to remember. "I think I said I tried to come up with an answer myself. No, wait. What did I say *exactly*?

"I know. I said I stayed up until *after twelve* trying to come up with an answer to the riddle."

"That's it!" Salem shouted.

CHAPTER 8

Tell me the *Golden Nile* exhibit is still at the museum!" Salem pleaded. "Please tell me it's still there!"

He had raced past Sabrina and into the kitchen, against all the new, outside-kitty rules.

Sabrina found him digging through the newspapers.

"I'm looking for the Arts Calendar!" he told her.

Sabrina didn't understand. "Why are we panicking?"

"Because I know the answer to the riddle!" Salem insisted. "And I need to say it to that jar so I can cure my bad luck. You've got to help me, Sabrina!"

"Here it is." Sabrina had the Arts Calendar open to the museum page. It had information about what was showing at each museum and theater around town.

"The *Golden Nile* show's still there," she reported. "Today's the last day, though."

Salem glared at the clock. "The museum closes at six," he snapped. "We don't have much time."

Just then the front door opened and Sabrina's aunts walked in.

"Salem!" Hilda gasped. "What are you doing inside the house?" Her face was frozen with fear as she slowly looked up. The chandelier above her head swayed.

Please don't fall, Salem thought.

"Sabrina, you've got to get him out of the house before something awful happens!" Zelda cried.

Salem noticed she'd been shopping. He worried about what she had in the bag. It looked like a *mirror*, for heaven's sake . . .

"Freeze!" Sabrina shouted. "Salem's got the answer to the riddle and we have to get to the museum right away before it closes so he can answer the jar and end the bad luck!"

Then she turned to Salem. "Did I get that right?"

It took a few seconds for Sabrina's message to sink in with Hilda and Zelda.

But they got it.

"What time does the museum close?" Zelda said.

"What time is it now?" Hilda said.

"We've got twenty minutes!" Salem shouted.

CHAPTER 9

Normally it took Zelda twenty minutes to get to the museum.

Hilda could get there in fifteen.

This time they took a witches' short-cut and got there in ten seconds.

"It really saves time to go as the crow flies," Zelda pointed out.

Now it was up to Salem to get inside the museum.

"It was a lot easier last time," Salem said with a worried frown. "People were going *in* the door. Now it's closing time, and everyone is coming *out*."

"What about a window?" Sabrina said. "Maybe there's one left open."

"It's raining, remember?" Salem griped. "All the windows are shut."

A guard walked by the door. It was almost closing time. "Stay back," Salem hissed. "I'm going in . . . alone."

"Hurry, Salem," Sabrina said as she opened the car door for him. "You only have one minute left!"

Salem jumped out of the car.

"Don't worry about me, kid," he said. "Everything's under control."

"Run!" Sabrina shouted.

But Salem did not run. He walked. Through the pouring rain.

"What's wrong with him!" Zelda said.

"It's raining like crazy! Why doesn't he get a move on!"

"Ruuuuuuuuuuun!" Hilda yelled. But her voice was drowned out by the cloudburst.

By the time he reached the top step to the front door of the museum Salem's coat was soaked.

He pressed his nose against the glass.

"Mewwwwwwwww!" he cried.

The shape of a guard appeared on the other side of the glass. Salem looked up and mewed again, woefully.

It was the guard with the bushy mustache.

Salem looked the guard in the eye and read the words on his lips through the glass: "Oh, kitty, kitty," the guard was saying.

Sabrina and her aunts saw it too.

"That guard's a sucker for cats," Sabrina said.

"And Salem's a great actor," Hilda said.

"I understand he's done some local dinner theater," Zelda said.

Salem's bluff was working.

The guard stuck a key in the lock and opened the door a crack.

"Hi there, kitty-kitty," said the guard.

Salem mewed.

"Does kitty-kitty need to come in and dry off?"

Salem mewed again.

"Awwwwwww!" the guard said at last, and pushed the door all the way open.

Salem edged in.

"That's better, isn't it? Hey—!"

Salem flew past him as if he'd been shot from a cannon.

"Come back here!"

CHAPTER 10

The exhibit halls were dark, but that was no problem for Salem. The only sound was the scritch-scritch of his claws tearing down the carpeted passageways.

Somewhere behind him the guard lumbered around, switching on the lights and calling, "Here kitty-kitty! Here kitty-kitty!"

Salem shot down the Hall of the Ancient Pyramids like a comet. The ancient monuments went by in a blur.

When he spotted the eyes of the Sphinx, he cut right and scrambled full speed ahead. He was still going flat out when the carpet ended and the floor changed to polished stone at the entrance to the Room of Jars.

Salem skated straight for the middle of the room. The riddle jar was dead ahead and coming up fast.

The riddle was ringing in his head.

What time is it when twelve cats chase a mouse?

Seconds before impact, Salem blurted out the answer.

"TWELVE AFTER ONE!" Salem cried.

And then he shut his eyes and felt the wind in his fur and waited to crash. Waited for the sound of ancient pottery breaking in a million pieces all over the floor.

But it never happened.

When Salem opened his eyes, there it was—the jar, the cats, the mouse, the riddle—everything looked the same as ever.

Somehow he'd stopped his slide across the floor just in time.

"Just lucky, I guess," he said.

CHAPTER 11

"Twelve after one!" Sabrina laughed. "I should have known!"

For days afterward Sabrina laughed about it.

Mostly she was relieved that things were back to normal.

Salem was living in the house again.

His luck had changed dramatically: his stocks were up nearly 15 percent.

He had Sabrina to thank for helping him solve the riddle and get to the museum.

"You kept the faith, Sabrina," he said.

"Don't mention it," Sabrina said.

But Salem wanted to be sure she knew how much he appreciated the way she'd stood by him.

"I got you a little something from the Metropolitan Museum," Salem said. "Mail order, of course."

"You shouldn't have," Sabrina said.

"Don't mention it," Salem said with a smile. "It wasn't very expensive. I get a discount for being a member."

Sabrina opened the little box, revealing a bright gold pin in the shape of a golden cat. It looked just like one of the statues in the Lair of Cats, where Sabrina had "rescued" Salem from her flash.

"Hey, cool!" Sabrina said. "Ow!"

"What happened?" Salem said.

Sabrina held up her finger where she'd poked it with the pin.

"Oh, bad luck," Salem said. As soon as the words left his lips, they both froze.

Their eyes locked.

"Did you say . . ." Sabrina started.

Salem threw up his paws. "Don't!" And he carefully pushed the cat pin back into its box.

"I think I'll get you some flowers, instead," he said.

And that was just fine with Sabrina.

Cat Care Tips

#1 Most adult cats can handle relatively cold and hot outdoor temperatures as long as they are used to being kept outside and have places where they can find shelter and shade.

#2 Cats should be kept inside under extreme winter or summer conditions.

#3 Remember, never leave your cat in a car in warm or hot weather.

#4 When it is cold outside, some outdoor cats

can get hurt because they climb into warm car engines. If you know there are outdoor cats in your neighborhood, you should check under the hood or in the wheel wells before you start a car that has been parked outside.

—Laura E. Smiley, MS, DVM, Dipl. ACVIM
Gwynedd Veterinary Hospital